Who Am I?

Written by **Julie Buchholtz** and Illustrated by **Aliya Ghare**

PUBLISHED by SLEEPING BEAR PRESS™

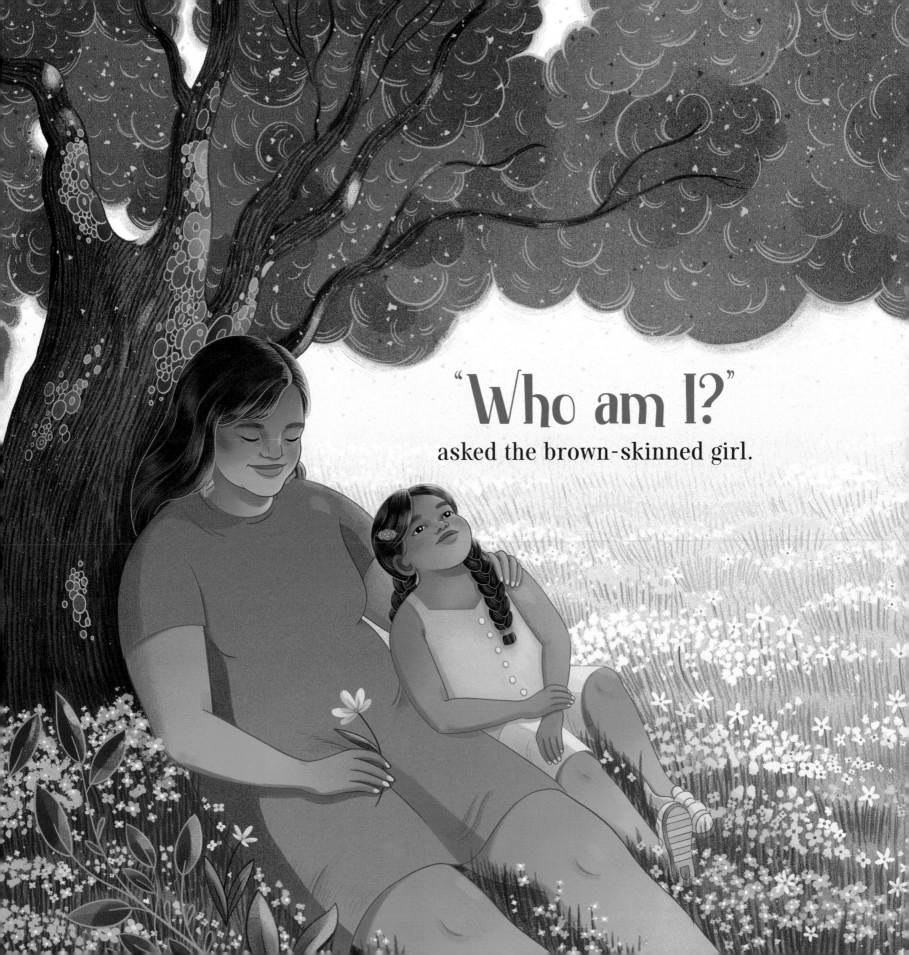

"Who am I?"

asked the brown-skinned girl.

Her big brown mama pulled
her close and replied—

You are the wind that scatters,
moving seeds across the field,
providing nourishment for our people.

You are the rain that falls,
quenching the thirsty land,
allowing new life to grow.

You are the fire that burns,
dancing flames of red and orange,
fending off the darkness.

"Who am I?"

asked the brown-skinned girl.

You are the eagle that flies,
soaring above the mountains,
connecting us to our ancestors.

You are the sun that shines,
warming the Earth,
coaxing our brothers and sisters from slumber.

You are the star that twinkles, brightening the midnight sky, bringing light and lending guidance.

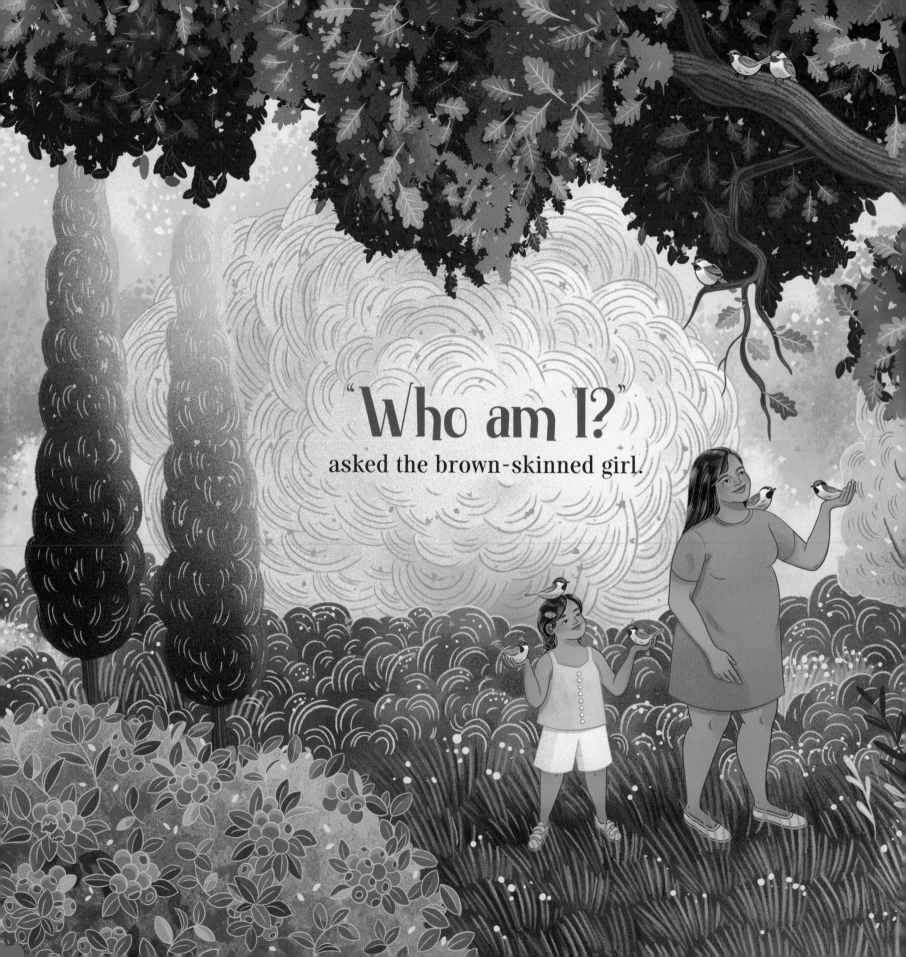

"Who am I?"

asked the brown-skinned girl.

You are the oak tree that stands,
serving as anchor,
offering safety and shelter.

You are the river that bends, winding and twisting, guiding along its path.

You are the wild rose that grows,
blooming in the spring,
coloring the world with beauty.

"Who am I?"
asked the brown-skinned girl.

You are the moon that glows,
waxing and waning,
marking the passage of time.

You are the snow that falls,
blanketing the ground,
protecting the soil and plants below.

You are the wolf that howls,

crying at the moon,

telling the story of our people.

While Big Brown Mama held her little brown
girl close, little brown girl listened.

Slowly, little brown girl's eyes grew sleepy,
her mouth curved into a smile—

I am the wind that scatters and the rain that falls.

I am the fire that burns and the eagle that flies.

I am the sun that shines and the star that twinkles.

I am the oak tree that stands and the river that bends.

I am the wild rose that grows and the moon that glows.

I am the snow that falls and the wolf that howls.

The little brown girl suddenly realized
that she was not so little after all.

Words From the Author

The little brown girl's final thought before she drifts off to sleep is the understanding of how she is connected to all of the animals, plants, and organisms on Mother Earth.

Do you know that YOU too are connected? In fact, we are ALL connected to one another and to this wonderful planet we call home or Mother Earth.

It is our job to take care of Mother Earth just as you would take care of yourself. Doing so will allow future generations to be safe, happy, and healthy.

To my one in a million husband, Larry; my very own mama, Linda; and my children.

—Julie

For the Indigenous children of Turtle Island, past and present.
And for my mom, whose love and spirit inspired the drawings in this book.

—Aliya

SLEEPING BEAR PRESS™

2395 South Huron Parkway, Suite 200
Ann Arbor, MI 48104
www.sleepingbearpress.com

Printed and bound in the United States.

10 9 8 7 6 5 4 3 2 1

Library of Congress Cataloging-in-Publication Data on file.

ISBN 9781534111813